To my mother and father, C.F.
For Angela, who made this story possible, S.J.P.

Text copyright © 1992 by Susie Jenkin-Pearce
Illustrations copyright © 1992 by Claire Fletcher
First published in Great Britain by The Bodley Head Children's Books. All rights reserved. No
part of this book may be reproduced or utilized in any form or by any means, electronic or
mechanical, including photocopying and recording, or by any information storage and
retrieval system, without permission in writing from the Publisher. Inquiries should be
addressed to Lothrop, Lee & Shepard Books, a division of William Morrow & Company, Inc.,
1350 Avenue of the Americas, New York, New York 10019. Printed and bound in Hong Kong.

First U.S. Edition   1 2 3 4 5 6 7 8 9 10

Library of Congress Cataloging in Publication data was not available in time for publication
of this book, but can be obtained from the Library of Congress.
ISBN 0-688-11725-2   ISBN 0-688-11726-0
L.C. Number 91-77296

THE SEASHELL SONG

*Susie Jenkin-Pearce and
Claire Fletcher*

Lothrop, Lee & Shepard Books

New York

As I was walking by the sea,
I found a shell, which sang to me;
it sang the story of the sea.

It sang the deep
of midnight black.

It sang the brilliance
of the sun.

It sang of storms.

It sang of calms.

It sang of ships
both great and small.

It sang of swarthy fishermen
and salty crews with mackerel nets.

It sang to me of long-ago gold,
spice and silk and minarets.

It sang of sailors all bewitched
by sirens' songs and mermaids' hair.

It sang of snow and arctic blue,
the northern lights, the frosty air.

It sang its song as it had done
a million times before.

I sat there filled with wonder,
a small child on the shore.